CELEBRATING U.S. HOLIDAYS

# Why Do We Celebrate THANKSGIVING?

Dorothy Jennings

**PowerKiDS press**

New York

Published in 2019 by The Rosen Publishing Group, Inc.
29 East 21st Street, New York, NY 10010

Copyright © 2019 by The Rosen Publishing Group, Inc.

All rights reserved. No part of this book may be reproduced in any form without permission in writing from the publisher, except by a reviewer.

First Edition

Editor: Brianna Battista
Book Design: Reann Nye

Photo Credits: Cover Bochkarev Photography/Shutterstock.com; p. 4 kali9/E+/Getty Images; p. 6 Everett Historical/Shutterstock.com; pp. 9, 24 American School/Getty Images; p. 10 https://commons.wikimedia.org/wiki/File:A_popular_history_of_the_United_States_-_from_the_first_discovery_of_the_western_hemisphere_by_the_Northmen,_to_%E2%80%A6; p 13 CCI ARCHIVES/Science Photo Library/Getty Images; p. 14 https://commons.wikimedia.org/wiki/File:Thanksgiving-Brownscombe.PNG; p. 17 KidStock/Blend Images/Getty Images; pp. 18, 24 Lyudmila Mikhailovskaya/Shutterstock.com; pp. 21, 24 a katz/Shutterstock.com; p. 22 Ariel Skelley/DigitalVision/Getty Images.

Cataloging-in-Publication Data

Names: Jennings, Dorothy.
Title: Why do we celebrate Thanksgiving? / Dorothy Jennings.
Description: New York : PowerKids Press, 2019. | Series: Celebrating U.S. holidays | Includes index.
Identifiers: LCCN ISBN 9781508166696 (pbk.) | ISBN 9781508166672 (library bound) | ISBN 9781508166702 (6 pack)
Subjects: LCSH: Thanksgiving Day–Juvenile literature.
Classification: LCC GT4975.J48 2019 | DDC 394.2649–dc23

Manufactured in the United States of America

CPSIA Compliance Information: Batch #CS18PK: For Further Information contact Rosen Publishing, New York, New York at 1-800-237-9932

# CONTENTS

A Fall Holiday　　　　　　　　　　4
The First Thanksgiving　　　　　　6
How We Celebrate　　　　　　　 18
Words to Know　　　　　　　　　24
Index　　　　　　　　　　　　　　24
Websites　　　　　　　　　　　　24

Thanksgiving is celebrated on the fourth Thursday of November.

5

6

Thanksgiving honors a **feast** that Native Americans shared with Pilgrims in 1621.

The Pilgrims were a group of European settlers. They came to America on a ship called the **Mayflower**.

9

10

Native Americans had lived in the Massachusetts area for a long time. The Pilgrims landed there in 1620.

Native Americans knew how to hunt and grow crops. They helped the Pilgrims live better.

13

14

The first Thanksgiving feast lasted three days. They ate foods such as corn, fish, and deer.

In 1941, Congress made Thanksgiving an official holiday.

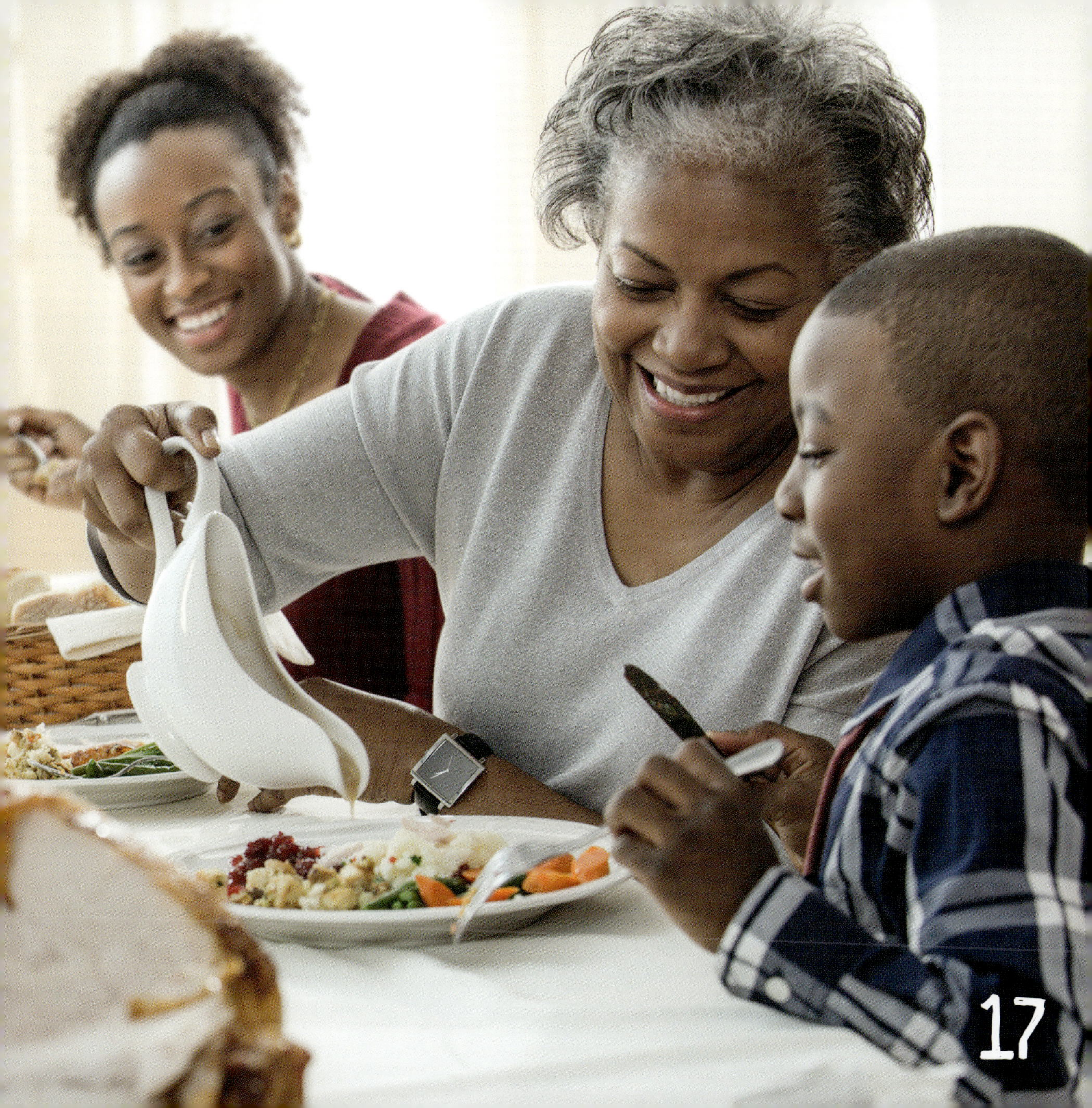

18

We celebrate Thanksgiving by eating dinner with our families and friends. Turkey and pumpkin pie are popular dishes.

The Thanksgiving Day **Parade** in New York City is one of the biggest parades in the world!

21

22

Thanksgiving honors America's history. How do you celebrate Thanksgiving with your family?

# Words to Know

feast

*Mayflower*

parade

# Index

**F**
feast, 7, 15

**M**
*Mayflower*, 8

**P**
parade, 20

# Websites

Due to the changing nature of Internet links, PowerKids Press has developed an online list of websites related to the subject of this book. This site is updated regularly. Please use this link to access the list: www.powerkidslinks.com/ushol/thank

3 1333 04778 6312